The pressure is on!

~~~

> **Longest Tail**
>
> **Biggest Ears**
>
> **Loudest Voice**
>
> **Best in Show**

Just then, my tummy jiggled and joggled.

Was that because of the bumpy road? Or was it because I was worried that I might not win a prize?

I didn't want to let down my friends in Room 26. After all, they were counting on me to win.

Look for all of

HUMPHREY'S TINY TALES

Humphrey's
Pet Show Panic

Betty G. Birney

illustrated by **Priscilla Burris**

PUFFIN BOOKS

To my sister and brother-in-law,
Janet and Steve Powell, and all the wonderful pets
they've had through the years
—B.B.

For Christina Tugeau and Christy Ewers,
with loving thoughts of Gertie, Jessie,
Trelle, and Peanut —P.B.

PUFFIN BOOKS
An imprint of Penguin Random House LLC
375 Hudson Street
New York, New York 10014

First published in the United States of America by G. P. Putnam's Sons.
Published by Puffin Books, an imprint of Penguin Random House LLC, 2018

Text copyright © 2018 by Betty G. Birney.
Illustrations copyright © 2018 by Priscilla Burris.

Library of Congress Cataloging-in-Publication Data
Names: Birney, Betty G., author. | Burris, Priscilla, illustrator.
Title: Humphrey's pet show panic / Betty G. Birney ; illustrated by Priscilla Burris.
Description: New York, NY : G. P. Putnam's Sons, [2018]
Summary: When a dog gets too close to Humphrey at the town pet show,
Og the Frog saves the day and Humphrey sees that having a great friend
is the best prize he could possibly win.
Identifiers: LCCN 2017004691 | ISBN 9781524737177 (hardcover)
Subjects: | CYAC: Hamsters—Fiction. | Pets—Fiction. | Pet shows—Fiction. | Friendship—Fiction.
Classification: LCC PZ7.B5229 Hsr 2018 | DDC [Fic]—dc23
LC record available at https://lccn.loc.gov/2017004691

Puffin Books ISBN 9781524737184

Printed in the United States of America.

1 3 5 7 9 10 8 6 4 2

Design by Eileen Savage.

Contents

Going to the Pet Show

"**H**ang on, Humphrey," A.J. said.

The car turned a corner and I slid across my cage.

"I'm trying!" I squeaked back.

Car rides aren't easy for hamsters like me. I don't even have a seat belt.

I'm the classroom hamster in Room 26 of Longfellow School. I

get to ride in cars a lot because I go home with a different student each weekend.

"This is my lucky day," A.J. told me. "Because Mrs. Brisbane picked *me* to bring you home for the weekend, I get to take you to the Pet Show."

A.J. and I had both been excited when Mrs. Brisbane told us about the Pet Show.

"This is your lucky day, too," A.J. told me. "You're going to win a prize!"

I crossed my paws and hoped he was right.

"Remember, A.J., Humphrey might not win," his mom said.

"There are lots of prizes," A.J. explained. "He's sure to win one of them. And I get to keep it!"

"Don't you have to share it with the class?" his grandmother asked.

"Humphrey's *my* pet," A.J. said. "At least for the weekend."

He pulled out a paper. "Here are the prizes," he said. He read the list out loud.

Friendliest

Best Trick

Most Unusual

Longest Tail

Biggest Ears

Loudest Voice

Best in Show

Just then, my tummy jiggled and joggled.

Was that because of the bumpy road? Or was it because I was worried that I might not win a prize?

I didn't want to let down my

friends in Room 26. After all, they were counting on me to win.

DeeLee, A.J.'s younger sister, giggled. "I think Humphrey should win for Best in Show!"

A.J.'s grandma turned around and looked in my cage. "He's one fine-looking hamster," she said.

"Thanks a lot!"
I said. But I'm
sure, like most
humans, all she
heard was "SQUEAK-
SQUEAK-SQUEAK."

I liked Grandma Grace.

I liked Grandma Grace's
purple hat, too.

Then the car stopped.

"Eeek!" I slid across the floor
of my cage.

"We're here," A.J.'s mom said.

"Yay!" A.J. shouted.

"Yay!" his younger brother Ty shouted.

"Yay!" DeeLee shouted.

"Goo! Goo!" his baby brother shouted.

"Eeek!" I squeaked quietly.

~~~~~

The Pet Show was held in a building in the middle of a park.

Outside, it was nice and quiet.

Inside, it was NOISY-NOISY-NOISY. And what noises there were!

Barking, meowing, chirping, snarling!

Yipping, yapping, squealing, shouting!

Someone called out, "Quiet, please!" But it still wasn't quiet.

"Here you go, Humphrey Dumpty," A.J. said as he set my cage on a table.

I like it when A.J. calls me Humphrey Dumpty. I call him Lower-Your-Voice-A.J. because his

voice is so loud. I have special names for all my friends in Room 26.

While A.J.'s family went to see the other pets, I looked around the room.

There was a lot to see, like dogs on leashes and cats in cages.

There was a lot to hear, like a screeching sound that made my whiskers wiggle and my tail twitch.

"BAWK!" a voice said. "Crackers is pretty!"

I wondered what kind of creature was such a screecher.

Next, a soft voice said, "Hi, A.J."

I looked up and saw Sayeh from Room 26. I call her Speak-Up-Sayeh because she is VERY-VERY-VERY quiet.

"Hi!" A.J.'s voice boomed.

Sayeh and her dad put a glass tank down next to me on the table.

"Og!" I squeaked. I was *so* happy to see my friend Og.

"I'm glad Mrs. Brisbane said I could bring him," Sayeh said. "I hope he wins a prize, too."

"BOING!" Og said.

He makes a very funny sound. He can't help it. He's a frog.

He's also my neighbor back in Room 26. His tank, which is half water and half land, sits right next to my cage.

Then A.J.'s best friend, Garth, showed up.

"Hi, Humphrey," Garth said. "I'm sure glad I could come see

you win a prize for our class! And Og, too."

A.J. said, "Remember, *I'm* the one who brought Humphrey."

Garth looked confused, but then another friend arrived.

Don't-Complain-Mandy Payne brought her pet hamster, Winky. Mandy's in Room 26, too. She doesn't complain as much since she got Winky.

"I think Winky will win Friendliest," she said.

"I just hope one of us wins a

prize," Winky squeaked to me from his cage.

"Me too," I said.

Winky is one of my friendliest friends, so I meant it. But I still didn't want to let A.J. down.

Richie showed up with a box with holes in the sides. Mrs. Brisbane always asks him to repeat his answers in class, so I call him Repeat-It-Please-Richie.

"Hi, everybody!" he said. "Want to see my new pet?"

"I do!" I squeaked.

A.J., Garth and Sayeh gathered around as Richie took the lid off the box.

"Meet Nick," Richie said.

Garth's eyes opened wide. "Wow!" he said.

"That's cool!" A.J. said.

"Amazing," Sayeh whispered.

What made Nick so amazing? All I could see was a box.

Richie put the box down next to me. My cage was between the box and Og's tank.

I leaned as far as I could to

look through one of the
hole. All I could see were
some leaves and twigs.

Was Nick invisible? Or had he
escaped?

"There's nothing in there," I
squeaked down to Og.

"BOING-BOING!" Og sounded
disappointed, too.

I was pretty sure that leaves and twigs couldn't win a prize at the Pet Show.

But I still wasn't sure I could win one, either.

The Show Begins

"The Pet Show is about to begin," a voice said.

I looked up at the stage. I was surprised to see that Carl was speaking. Carl worked at Pet-O-Rama, the shop where I lived before I came to Room 26.

"Hi, Carl!" I squeaked.

He couldn't hear me over the yipping, yapping, screeching and snarling.

"Bawk! Crackers will win!" the screecher said. "Bawk!"

I was already pretty sure Crackers would win the prize for Loudest Voice.

Carl introduced the judges for the Pet Show.

The first judge was Dr. Ginger Jones. She was a vet. That's a

22

doctor for animals. She smiled and waved to the crowd.

The second judge was Stormy Sanchez. He was the weather reporter from TV. He smiled and waved to the crowd.

The third judge was a real judge. A justice of the peace.

Judge Wong waved to the crowd, but he didn't smile.

Then the judges went to look at the cats.

I heard a lot of meowing, growling and hissing. I was glad to be far away from all that noise!

Richie leaned down and spoke to Nick. "Don't worry, Nick. You're sure to win."

Who *was* this Nick, anyway? Why was Richie so sure he would win?

"Og, maybe
if I got up higher, I
could see him," I said.

I scrambled to the top of my
ladder. I jumped onto my tree
branch and climbed up to the
very top.

Then I carefully got up on my tippy toes and grabbed the top bars of the cage.

Paw over paw, I worked my way to the corner. When I looked down, I felt a little dizzy. But maybe this could win the prize for Best Trick!

I could see inside the box. But after all that climbing, all I saw was that same pile of old leaves and twigs.

Was Richie playing a trick on the judges?

"There's still nothing there, Og," I squeaked to my friend.

Og splashed around in the water in his tank, but I knew he was disappointed.

"And now, the Parade of Pooches," Carl announced.

The owners brought their dogs to the center of the room. Luckily, they were on leashes.

I must admit, I've been a bit afraid of dogs ever since I came nose to nose with a RUDE-RUDE-RUDE one named Clem.

The dogs and their humans walked around in a circle while Carl introduced them.

One puppy named Oscar was LONG-LONG-LONG, but his legs

were SHORT-
SHORT-SHORT.
He looked like a
giant hot dog.

Then there was a tall, spotted dog named Smoky, who held his head high. He walked when his human walked and stopped when his human stopped. When his owner said, "Heel," Smoky followed right at her heels. Good dog!

Next came
a   teeny-tiny
dog named Cha-Cha. Her legs
moved very fast to keep up with
her human.

 Doodles was a
shaggy dog with
no eyes at all. At
least I couldn't
see any under all
that fur. But he seemed to know
where he was going.

Then my heart suddenly went
THUMPITY-THUMP-THUMP.

I didn't need to hear Carl

say the next
dog's name.
I'd know that

big nose anywhere!

It was Miranda's dog, Clem.

I love Golden-Miranda. That's
what I call her, but her name
is really Miranda Golden. She is
one of my favorite friends from
Room 26.

But I don't love Clem. I met him
when I went to Miranda's house
for a weekend. I still remembered
his large, sharp teeth and his
smelly doggy breath.

As Miranda led him around the circle, the judges made notes.

"Next, the other pets," Carl announced.

Other pets? Did that mean Og and me?

"Bawk! Crackers will win!" a voice screeched.

I hopped onto my wheel and started spinning.

"The judges are coming, Og," I told my friend. "Be friendly, splash around, make some noise!"

I didn't hear a thing coming from his cage.

Why was Og so quiet? Didn't he want to win a prize? Did he want to let our friends down?

The judges walked toward our table.

"Remember, we're here to win, Og," I squeaked. "It's showtime!"

~~~~~

First, the judges looked at a creature called a bearded dragon. Eeek!

I thought dragons breathed fire and ate people. But this

dragon turned out to be a fancy lizard named Lola.

"She's very unusual," Stormy Sanchez said.

"Very," Dr. Jones agreed.

"Hmm," Judge Wong said. He wrote something in a little notebook.

Then the judges looked at a guinea pig, a turtle, and a rabbit named Peter.

Next, they moved to my friend Winky's cage. Winky was born with one eye closed, so he always looked as if he was winking.

"Wow, he's friendly!" the vet said.

Suddenly, that awful voice screeched, "Crackers is pretty! Crackers will win."

Now I could see Crackers, sitting on her human's arm. She was a huge bird with green and yellow feathers. And she was quite pretty.

"Ah, a parrot!" Judge Wong said, looking at Crackers.

Stormy Sanchez nodded. "A fine-looking bird."

The girl who owned her said,

"Sing,
Crackers!"

The crowd all cheered when Crackers sang, "La-la-la!"

I liked Crackers's singing. I didn't like her large, sharp beak.

As the judges headed toward our end of the table, my tummy felt jumpy and jiggly again.

I heard Garth tell A.J., "I know Humphrey's going to win a prize."

"Of course he will," A.J. said, but he sounded worried.

Maybe he wasn't really sure I could win.

To squeak the truth, neither was I.

Here Come
the Judges

First, the judges stopped at Og's tank.

"Show them what a great frog you are, Og," I told my friend. "Do your very best."

Everyone stared at Og.

Og looked at the judges, but he didn't do anything else.

"BOING for them, Oggy!" I squeaked.

But Og didn't BOING. He didn't even splash.

He just stared at the judges.
They stared back.

"Come on, Og," whispered
Sayeh. "Show them what a good
swimmer you are."

Og kept on staring.

What did Og see? I looked out at the crowd.

I saw people, dogs, cats, dragons, birds and other strange creatures. Maybe Og was scared.

"Don't be afraid, Og!" I said. "Act friendly! Say hello!"

"BOING!" he said at last.

Stormy Sanchez looked surprised. "What was that?" he asked.

"That's how he talks," Garth explained.

"BOING-BOING!" Og jumped up and down.

The judges leaned in and looked more interested. But then Crackers opened her beak and started squawking again.

"Crackers is the best!" she said.

Then Og stopped. He didn't make another sound.

At least he'd tried. A little.

The judges moved on to my cage. Now it was all up to me.

"Who's this?" Stormy Sanchez asked.

"Humphrey," A.J. said. "He's a Golden Hamster."

I was ready to put on a great show.

First, I leaped up to the side of my cage, looked straight at the judges and squeaked, "Hello!"

"He's a friendly little fellow!" Stormy exclaimed.

Next, I hopped onto my wheel and did a fast spin.

"Look at him go!" said Dr. Jones.

I climbed back up to the top of my cage and grabbed the highest bar. With just one paw holding

on, I swung back
and forth.

Sometimes,
I amaze myself.

"Goodness,"
Judge Wong said.

Next, I slid
DOWN-DOWN-DOWN
and dropped back onto the wheel.
This time, I spun backward!

My whiskers were wilting, but
I kept on spinning. The judges
made notes.

"Great job," said Dr. Jones.

I was very proud.

Then she noticed the box next to me. "What's in there?" she asked.

"That's Nick," Richie said. "I'll make him move."

The judges came closer as Richie poked around inside the box.

I stopped spinning so I could watch.

Even Judge Wong looked surprised. "I thought it was a stick until it moved," he said.

I thought I saw a stick move

in there, too. But a stick doesn't move all by itself, does it?

"It's a stick insect," Richie explained. "That's why I call him Nick—Nick the Stick."

People crowded around to see Nick.

"The stick is an insect!" I squeaked to Og.

"BOING-BOING!" Og twanged loudly.

He was probably excited because he likes insects. He likes them for dinner. And breakfast, too. Yuck!

"BOING-BOING-BOING!" Og repeated.

People in the crowd laughed.

"Og has a pretty loud voice," A.J. said.

I guess he still hoped that Og could win a prize.

So did I. But I wasn't sure he was louder than the screeching parrot.

Next, Carl asked the owners to bring pets with special tricks to the center of the room.

Smoky, the spotted dog, rolled over and sat up and begged.

Cha-Cha, the tiny dog, stood on her hind legs and did a hula dance. At least that's what her owner called it.

Oscar, the hot-dog pup, sang. It was more of a wail than singing.

Crackers tried to drown him out by singing, "La-la-la."

It was NOISY-NOISY-NOISY.

But I was still wondering about Nick. He didn't look like any kind of insect I'd ever seen. And what kind of stick can move by itself?

Luckily, I have a secret lock-that-doesn't-lock. It allows me to get in and out of my cage without humans knowing.

So while everyone watched the tricks, I jiggled the lock.

As the door swung open, I saw Miranda lead Clem to the center of the room.

I didn't think Clem was clever enough to do a trick, but it turned out he could chase his own tail. I was just glad he wasn't chasing *me*.

While all eyes were on Clem, I tiptoed over to Nick's box. I couldn't see over the top, but there were air holes in the side of the box. I got up on my tiptoes and peeked inside.

What a
strange sight!

Nick still looked like a stick, but now I saw that the stick had eyes! And it had twiggy little legs that moved!

"Eeek!" I squeaked.

I was sure no one heard me because the crowd was so noisy.

I looked over and saw that the people were cheering for a cat.

"I never heard of a cat doing tricks," A.J. told Garth.

"Me neither," Garth replied.

But this cat did a great trick. His owner had a big hoop and the cat leaped right through it.

Then he turned around and
leaped through it again!

The trick was so amazing, I
forgot I was out of my cage.

Then something happened that made me forget about Nick the Stick.

I wasn't worried about winning a prize anymore.

I was only worried about staying alive!

A Matter of Life and Breath

When the dogs saw the performing cat, they got excited. I'd never heard so much barking, howling, yipping and yapping in my life.

But Clem was more excited than any of them.

"Stay!" Miranda yelled as Clem tugged at his leash.

She tried to stop him, but he pulled the leash right out of her hand. He rushed toward the cat.

As the cat jumped through the hoop again, Clem jumped right after him!

Just then a strange thing happened. Clem stopped chasing the cat and he sniffed the air. I'm not sure what he smelled, but he headed straight for me!

That's when I remembered I was out of my cage. And if Clem got to me before I got back inside, I'd be in big trouble!

"BOING-BOING-BOING!" Og was scared for me, too. But there wasn't much he could do to help.

Just as I reached my cage, Clem's big nose poked up over the edge of the table.

I saw his sharp, shiny teeth.

I smelled his horrible doggy breath.

"Bad dog!" Miranda shouted.

I heard Og splashing wildly and BOING-ing.

"Somebody stop that dog!" Carl shouted.

"Humphrey's out of the cage!" A.J. bellowed.

"Grab him!" Garth yelled. "Quick!"

Before anyone could grab me,
I saw Clem's big paws on the
table. His jaws opened wide.

Eeek! I took a flying leap and
landed on his long nose.

Clem's eyes crossed as
he tried to look
at me.

I scrambled up his nose to the place between his ears. Clem didn't like that, so he shook his head—hard. I hung on to a clump of his fur for dear life.

Just then, Og leaped up out of his tank, popping the plastic top right off. He landed next to me on the top of Clem's head!

Clem seemed VERY-VERY-VERY confused. I don't think he'd ever had a hamster and a frog on his head before.

He lowered his head and shook it again.

Og and I slid straight down to
the floor!

"Run, Og! Hurry!" I squeaked
as I raced away from Clem.

My heart was pounding. We hopped and ran under the table and out again. We were weaving between people's big feet and past rows of cages. There was panic all around us, but no one was more scared than I was.

"Bad dog! Come back!" That was Miranda.

"Bad dog—bawk!" That was
Crackers.

"Woof!" "Yip!" "Meow!" That
was from all the other pets.

"Somebody stop that dog!"
That was Carl again.

I could smell Clem's awful
doggy breath and knew he was
close behind.

Suddenly, everything went dark. Og and I kept racing ahead, but I couldn't see a thing.

Then the world turned upside down. Og and I were flipped up, down and all around.

"I've got them!" a voice called out.

"Eeek!" I squeaked.

Finally, I could see light again.

"A hat always comes in handy," Grandma Grace said.

She was smiling down at us. I didn't know who she was at first,

because she wasn't wearing her
purple hat.

I quickly figured out what had
happened. She had thrown the
hat over us, then scooped us up.

Og and I were inside Grandma Grace's hat!

That purple hat saved our lives.

"Thanks, Grandma Grace," I squeaked weakly.

"Boing!" Og sounded pretty tired, too.

Lots of humans gathered around to look at us, but Grandma Grace shooed them away. "Let these little fellows rest," she said.

I liked Grandma Grace and her purple hat VERY-VERY-VERY much.

Soon I was back in my cage and Og was splashing in his tank.

Then the judges stepped forward to tell us the winners of the prizes.

My tummy did a flip-flop. I hoped my friends wouldn't be too disappointed if I didn't win a prize.

"It was a tough choice," Stormy Sanchez said.

"We think you're all winners," Dr. Jones said.

"Let's hand out the ribbons," Judge Wong said.

I crossed my toes as they awarded the prizes.

The Best Trick prize went to the cat who jumped through the hoop. His name was Noodles.

Peter the Rabbit won the Biggest Ears prize. That was no surprise!

The prize for the Longest Tail went to Clem.

I suppose he did have the longest tail, but I wouldn't have given him a prize for anything.

Still, I was happy for Miranda.

Crackers won the prize for the Loudest Voice.

"Crackers is the best!" the parrot squawked.

She was loud, all right. I just wished that sometimes she'd keep her beak shut.

"There were two winners for Most Unusual Pet," Stormy Sanchez said.

My ears pricked up. Maybe Og would get a prize here.

But the two
winners were
Nick the Stick
and Lola the Bearded Dragon.

Og had lost to a bearded lady and a stick!

I was happy for Richie, though. He jumped up and down and high-fived his friends.

"I'm sure you'll win the next prize, Humphrey," A.J. whispered to me.

I noticed that A.J. had his fingers crossed, so I crossed my paws as well as my toes.

Stormy Sanchez announced another prize with two winners. "The prizes for Friendliest Pet go to Winky and Humphrey," he said.

I could hardly believe my tiny ears.

"BOING-BOING!" Og twanged.

Everybody cheered and I was HAPPY-HAPPY-HAPPY to share the prize with Winky.

"I won!" A.J. shouted. "I get the prize!"

"No, *Humphrey* won," Garth said. "He's the class pet of everybody in Room Twenty-six. Why should you get the prize?"

A.J. shook his head. "Because I'm the one who . . ."

But A.J. didn't finish the sentence. He opened his mouth to say something, but then he closed it again.

He was unusually quiet . . . for A.J. He stared at Garth and Sayeh for a few seconds and looked a little sad.

"I guess you're right," he told them.

When he and Mandy stepped up to accept the prizes, A.J. asked if he could say something.

Stormy handed him the microphone. Not that A.J. needed one with his loud voice.

"This prize is for everybody in Room Twenty-six," he said. "Humphrey is our classroom

hamster, so he belongs to us all. Hooray for Humphrey!"

Everyone clapped, including me. I was PROUD-PROUD-PROUD of A.J. for sharing!

The judges gave the prize

for Best in Show to Smoky, the spotted dog. The crowd cheered and I joined in.

I thought all the prizes had been awarded, but the judges weren't finished.

"We are also giving a very special prize that was not on the list," Stormy Sanchez said with a big smile on his face. "Og the Frog gets the prize for Best Friend, for helping Humphrey."

Og won a special prize for helping me!

Sayeh looked very proud and so did my other friends from Room 26. Stormy handed the microphone to her.

If there's one thing Sayeh doesn't like, it's speaking in front of other people. But in her soft voice, she said, "Thank you. I will share this with my classmates, because Og is also the pet of everyone in Room Twenty-six."

As the crowd clapped, my friends started chanting, "Og, Og, Og, Og!"

No one squeaked louder than I did.

When things quieted down again, Stormy Sanchez said, "We'd also like to thank Mrs. Grace Cook. Thanks for your quick thinking and your purple hat."

Grandma Grace waved to the cheering crowd.

My tiny paws were getting sore from clapping!

When the cheering stopped, I turned to Og. "THANKS-THANKS-THANKS for helping me."

Og dived to the bottom of his tank. Then he did three backward somersaults.

It was a prize-winning trick, but no one saw it except me.

Home Sweet Home

On the way to the car, A.J. seemed quieter than usual.

"What's the matter?" asked Grandma Grace. "You're not usually so quiet."

"I just wish I could get a pet,"

he said. "But Dad says not right now."

I wished he could, too. He always took GOOD-GOOD-GOOD care of me.

"You already have a great pet," Grandma said. "He's right here. And he's got a big, shiny ribbon!"

A.J. sighed. "But I have to share Humphrey with everyone in Room Twenty-six."

Grandma chuckled. "You have to share me, too."

It was true. A.J. had to share his grandma with his brothers and sister.

"But you know how much I love you," Grandma said. "I'll bet Humphrey feels the same way about you."

Grandma Grace was one smart human.

"It's TRUE-TRUE-TRUE," I squeaked.

A.J. laughed. "Humphrey Dumpty, you're funny. I'm lucky you're my class pet. And Og, too."

That made me feel even better than winning a prize at the Pet Show.

~~~

A.J. couldn't wait for us to go back to school on Monday. He wanted to show my ribbon to our teacher, Mrs. Brisbane.

He was PROUD-PROUD-PROUD. So was I.

Everybody wanted to tell Mrs. Brisbane about what had happened at the Pet Show.

"It was so funny to see that purple hat running across the floor with Humphrey and Og under it," Garth said.

"It looked silly," Mandy said. "But it was terrible that Humphrey was in danger."

When I heard the word "danger," I let out a loud "Eeek!"

"But it was wonderful that Og was so brave and helped him," Mandy continued.

Miranda looked as if she was about to cry. "Oh, I feel horrible. My dog could have hurt Humphrey, or worse!" she said. "I'm so sorry."

She looked really upset. I felt sorry for her, even if Clem was a truly awful dog.

By the way, doesn't Pet-O-Rama sell breath mints for dogs?

"I hope you stay in your cage from now on," Mrs. Brisbane

said. "I don't want anything bad
to happen to you."

"Me either," I agreed.

"Richie, maybe you can bring
Nick the Stick in one day for
our science class," Mrs. Brisbane
continued.

"Sure," said Richie. "Anytime!"

"Hey, what do you get if you cross a stick insect with a parrot?" Kirk asked.

Mrs. Brisbane shook her head. "I don't know, Kirk. What?"

"A walkie-talkie!" he said with a grin.

The thought of Crackers crossed with an insect like Nick made me laugh.

It made everyone else in Room 26 laugh, too.

~~~

At the end of the day, Og and I were alone in Room 26.

I looked at the shiny ribbon hanging on my cage.

I looked at the shiny ribbon hanging on Og's tank.

"I'm glad we won prizes, Og," I told him. "We made our friends happy."

Og splashed around in the water.

Then I continued, "But I don't really need a prize. Because being a classroom pet is the BEST-BEST-BEST job in the world!"

"BOING-BOING-BOING!" Og twanged.

Even though I don't really understand frog talk, I was pretty sure that he agreed with me.

Best
Class
Pets